Stuck in
the Middle

Tom Tinn-Disbury

Tilly lived in the mountains with her mummy and daddy.
She loved it there. There was plenty of space for her to run and play.

The rolling hills went on for miles and miles and she was surrounded by all sorts of animals. There were sheep, cows, and even a goat.

The only thing Tilly didn't like was that they didn't all live together.

For some of the time, Tilly lived on one mountain with Mummy.

Then, for the rest of the time, she lived on another mountain with Daddy.

The two mountains were
joined by a long, wobbly bridge.

There was also a dense, thick fog
surrounding the bridge that
never seemed to go away.

Mummy and Daddy always found reasons for why they couldn't use the bridge.

Tilly just wanted them all to meet in the middle.

Instead, Tilly had to make the long, winding trek down one mountain.

Then she had to make the slow, plodding climb up the other mountain every week. This made Tilly really grumpy and tired.

After a long time of going back

and forth,

forth

and back,

up

and down,

down

and up,

Tilly had finally had enough.

Why did Mummy and Daddy
have to live so far apart?

Why did they never do
things together anymore,
like other families do?

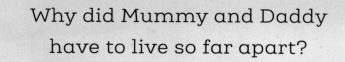

Tilly began to think that
maybe she could be the reason.

What could she do to fix it?

Then, Tilly had an idea...

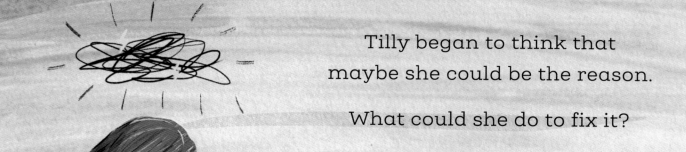

Maybe if she could repair the old,
wobbly bridge then they could
all meet in the middle.

There would be no more
long, winding treks.
No more feeling tired and grumpy.
Instead, there would be more
time to spend together.

Just as it got dark, Tilly packed
her bag and snuck out of the
house, ready to fix things.

She couldn't wait to surprise Mummy and Daddy in the morning!

At night time the bridge looked really dark and scary.

It was swaying in the howling wind,

and the fog was still thick and heavy.

"I'll be ok," Tilly thought to herself. "I'll just go really
slowly and carefully, and the torch will light my way."

She started one step at a time, fixing and repairing as best she could. Slowly, Tilly made her way along the bridge. Until, before she knew it, she was in the middle.

Halfway.

Tilly let out a deep sigh of relief. But, as she was fixing the bridge she realised that the fog was getting thicker. Now, even with the torch, she couldn't see in front or behind her.

Tilly was stuck. Stuck in the middle.

Tilly didn't know what to do.
She just stood still, closed her eyes, and began to sob.

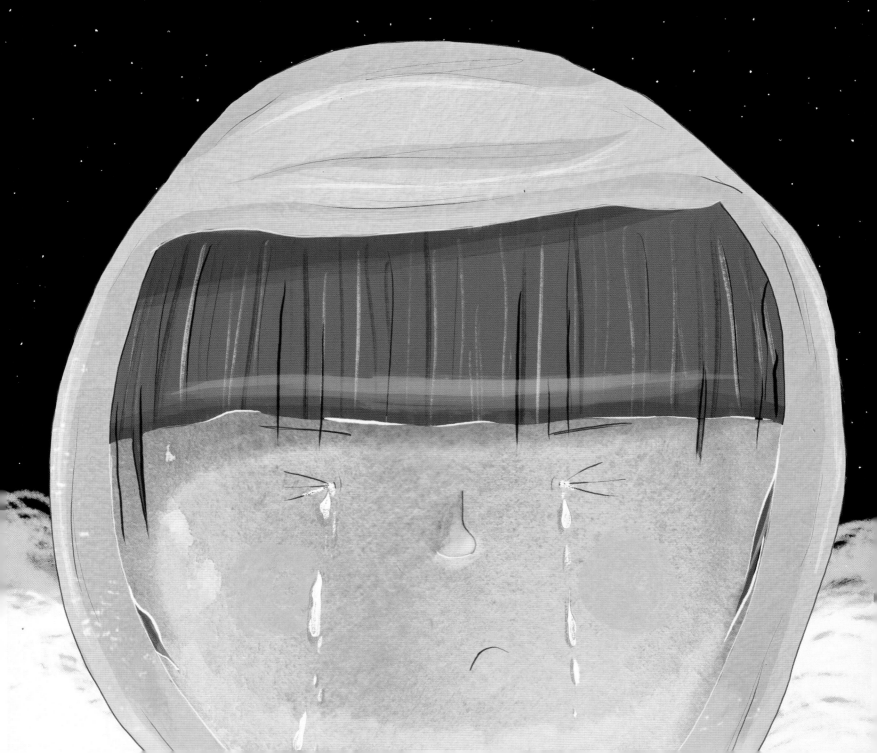

After what felt like forever,
Tilly heard a noise. Then she heard
it again. It was getting louder.

It was Mummy and Daddy.
They were coming to get her.

"Tilly, don't move!"
cried Mummy.

"We're coming to get you!"
shouted Daddy.

Tilly's mummy and daddy worked together
and met her in the middle of the bridge.

Then she had something that she hadn't had in a long time...
a really big hug from both of them. At the same time.

With that, all the fog lifted and they made their way off the bridge.

"What were you doing crossing the
bridge, Tilly? asked Daddy.

"I was trying to fix it so that we didn't have to go up and
down the mountains anymore," sobbed Tilly. "Then maybe
we would have more time to spend together as a family."

"Nothing is broken here, Tilly. And if it
was, it certainly isn't your job to fix it!"
Mummy comforted her.

"But I feel like I am the reason that you
don't live together anymore!" sighed Tilly.

"There might be a few reasons why we
don't live in the same house, but it will
never be you," Daddy said.

"It is ok to feel angry, sad, or even guilty, Tilly. I know that us living apart is hard, but you know you can talk to us whenever you need to," continued Mummy.

"Or if you don't want to talk to us, there are lots of other people who will support and listen to you, like your friends, teachers, or Grandma and Grandpa," reassured Daddy.

"Anyway, living apart isn't *all* bad…" said Mummy with a smile.

"You have two bedrooms to snuggle up in…"

"Two kitchens to make a mess in…" said Daddy.

"Even two pets to play with…" giggled Tilly.

"That's two homes full of love!" agreed Mummy and Daddy.

"Our love for you is one of the things that will always bring us together," reassured Daddy.

"You're the bridge between us."

Brought together by their love for
Tilly, Mummy and Daddy worked
hard to make the journey between
them a simple and safe one.

Mummy and Daddy may still live mountains apart,
but now, Tilly feels closer to them than ever.

Guide for Grown-Ups

Going through a divorce or separation can be difficult, not only on you but on your child, too.

What should I tell my child?

- Remind them that they are loved by you both.

- Be as honest as you can about what has happened and what this will mean for the future.

- Use simple, age-appropriate language to explain everything, so that it is easier for your child to understand. You may need to have the same conversation a number of times as your child develops.

- Listen to your child and answer any questions they may have. It is okay if you don't know all of the answers right now, but it is important that they feel heard by you.

- Make sure that your child knows that they can talk to you whenever they need to. Even if you are not living together, it is important that they know that you are still reachable and will always be there for them.

- Make sure your child knows that if they don't want to talk to you, there are others that will support them, including friends, family, and teachers.

- Ensure they know that the situation isn't their fault and reassure them that it is okay to show and feel a range of emotions.

What else can I do to help them?

- Tackle the conversation together, if possible. This reiterates that while you may be separated, you are still parenting as a unit and will remain a family.

- Children like routines, so make them aware of how this will change and try to keep things as normal as possible.

- Try not to argue or talk negatively about the other parent, especially in front of your child.

- Remember you are parenting together, so make sure you are both on the same page. It is important to work collaboratively and ensure you support each other.

- Seek professional support if you are worried about your child, or if you are finding it hard to co-parent together.

Resources:

- YoungMinds – An organisation that provides reassurance and support to young people who are struggling.

- Relate – An organisation that provides family counselling and advice on understanding children's feelings and actions during separation.

- Families Need Fathers – A charity that helps children and families to retain positive relationships after divorce or separation.

- Two Wishes – An international organisation that offers information and advice on how to maintain healthy family relationships for parents going through a separation.

Penguin Random House

Created for DK by Plum5 Ltd

Consultant Angharad Rudkin
Editor Abi Luscombe
Designer Brandie Tully-Scott
Special Sales & Custom Executive Isobel Walsh
Publisher Francesca Young
Deputy Art Director Mabel Chan
Publishing Director Sarah Larter
Production Editor Dragana Puvacic
Production Controller John Casey

First published in Great Britain in 2023 by
Dorling Kindersley Limited
DK, One Embassy Gardens, 8 Viaduct Gardens,
London, SW11 7BW

The authorised representative in the EEA is
Dorling Kindersley Verlag GmbH. Arnulfstr.
124, 80636 Munich, Germany

A CIP catalogue record for this book is
available from the British Library.
ISBN: 978-0-2415-7500-0

Printed and bound in China

MIX
Paper | Supporting
responsible forestry
FSC™ C018179

This book was made with Forest Stewardship
Council™ certified paper – one small step in
DK's commitment to a sustainable future.
For more information go to
www.dk.com/our-green-pledge

For the curious

www.dk.com

About Tom Tinn-Disbury

Tom Tinn-Disbury lives and works in Warwickshire with his wife, two children, and (ever growing) menagerie of animals: cats, Sparky and Loki, and dogs, Wilma and Bill. He uses a mix of pencils, paint, and computers to create his art, and coffee and sandwiches to write his stories.

Tom has attempted to tackle the big and sometimes complex subjects in a way that helps children and adults alike. He hopes this book will spark a conversation and then perhaps be a starting point for families on their journey to resolution.

Tom would like to dedicate this book to all the families grown from the seeds of separation.

About Dr. Angharad Rudkin

Dr. Angharad Rudkin is a consultant and Clinical Psychologist. An expert on complicated family circumstances, Dr. Rudkin has worked with children, young people, and families for over 20 years.

Angharad has used her experience to contribute to multiple books that aim to help young people and their families.

Struggling children, like Tilly, have taught her about the importance of honesty and resilience.